# The Adventures of NICKELODEON JIMMY NEUTRON BOY GENIUS

# Love Potion

by Steven Banks       illustrated by Natasha Sasic

Simon Spotlight/Nickelodeon
New York  London  Toronto  Sydney

Based on the TV series *The Adventures of Jimmy Neutron, Boy Genius*® as seen on Nickelodeon®

SIMON SPOTLIGHT
An imprint of Simon & Schuster Children's Publishing Division
1230 Avenue of the Americas, New York, NY 10020
Copyright © 2004 Viacom International Inc. All rights reserved. NICKELODEON,
*The Adventures of Jimmy Neutron, Boy Genius*, and all related titles, logos, and
characters are trademarks of Viacom International Inc. All rights reserved,
including the right of reproduction in whole or in part in any form.
SIMON SPOTLIGHT and colophon are registered trademarks of Simon & Schuster.
Manufactured in the United States of America
First Edition  10 9 8 7 6 5 4 3 2 1
ISBN 0-689-86317-9

Jimmy Neutron held up a bottle of pinkish fluid toward his friends Carl and Sheen.

"Gentlemen, this may be my most dangerous experiment yet! More powerful than a superpowered jet, more lethal than an orbiting space laser . . . I give you pheromone number 99!"

Carl and Sheen stared at the bottle in horror.

"It's terrifying!" Carl exclaimed, and then he paused. "What's a pheromone?"

"It's a chemical hormone that makes boys like girls. One whiff of this will make a guy fall in love with the first girl he sees," explained Jimmy.

"You're a madman! It's got to be destroyed!" cried Sheen as he tried to grab the bottle.

"No, Sheen," said Jimmy. "I'm going to use it to invent an *anti-girl vaccine.*"

"Oh," replied Sheen, "I've obviously misjudged you."

Jimmy carefully stored the pheromone in the containment chamber. "I'll keep it in here until the vaccine is fully finished."

After the pheromone was safely stored Carl sat down at Jimmy's computer.

"Jimmy, can I check my e-mail?" asked Carl. "I want to see if my Cheese of the Month is on its way."

Then, without realizing it, Carl pushed the wrong button and accidentally released some of the love serum into the air! None of the boys noticed that the containment chamber had opened.

Jimmy needed to go to the science store to get some more supplies for the anti-girl vaccine. He agreed to meet Carl and Sheen back at the lab in one hour.

"See you guys later!" said Sheen as he ran out of the lab to go home to watch Ultra Lord on TV.

"Okey-dokey," said Carl. "I'll hang around and see if Jimmy's mom is making any cookies."

While walking to the store Jimmy bumped into the most annoying girl in Retroville: Cindy Vortex.

"Hey, Nerdtron," said Cindy. "Invent anything stupid today?"

Jimmy opened his mouth and couldn't believe what he said: "Gee, Cindy, you look absolutely beautiful!"

Cindy backed away from Jimmy. "See you later, Neutron . . . when you're not crazy!"

On his way home to watch Ultra Lord, Sheen spotted his classmate, Libby.

"My beautiful Queen of the Galaxy," cried Sheen. "Your wish is my command!"

"Sheen, you are too weird!" said Libby. "I'm out of here!"

Libby ran away, but Sheen chased after her. "Wait, my Queen! Your loyal subject bids you to command him!"

Back at Jimmy's house Carl walked into the kitchen and saw Mrs. Neutron making cookies.

"Hello, Carl," said Mrs. Neutron. "Would you like a cookie?"

"I would, Mrs. Neutron," said Carl. "And I would also like to spend eternity with you!"

After seeing Cindy, Jimmy felt very strange. Everywhere he looked he saw her!

"What's wrong with me?" he wondered. "I can't stop thinking about Cindy Vortex! I must find her and figure out what's going on!"

"My sweet Libby!" shouted Sheen. "I want to prove my love for you by performing the Arcturian Dance of Wooing from Episode 921, 'The Courtship of Ultra Lord's Father!'"

Sheen began to do a goofy dance. Libby was so embarrassed that she made Sheen come inside so the neighbors wouldn't see him.

Jimmy found Cindy at the Candy Bar.

"I can't get you out of my mind!" Jimmy said, pressing his nose against the window.

"What is your problem, Nerdtron?" demanded an embarrassed Cindy.

Jimmy couldn't believe what he said next. "My problem is that . . . I love you, Cindy Vortex!"

Cindy couldn't believe her ears! Jimmy Neutron said he *loved* her!

"Okay, Neutron!" said Cindy. "Meet me in the alley! Now!"

Once outside Cindy cornered Jimmy in the alley behind the
Candy Bar.

"Okay, Neutron! What is going on?" she asked suspiciously.

Jimmy looked at her with lovesick eyes. "Would you like to come
back to my lab with me for a date?"

"A date with you?" answered Cindy. "Okay. But if this is a trick
you'll have to go back in time to make sure you were never born!"

With that, they walked off toward Jimmy's lab.

Back in Libby's living room Sheen prepared himself to ask her an important question. "Will you marry me, O Shining One?" asked Sheen.

"Whoa! Time out! Slow down!" said Libby. "We are *not* getting married!"

"But I thought every girl dreamed of an Ultra Lord-themed wedding?" asked Sheen.

Libby pushed Sheen out the door. "Not this girl!"

"Have I displeased my goddess?" asked Sheen. "Was it my breath?"

Libby shook her head. "Look, Sheen, I've got homework. You're kind of cute in a strange sort of way. We'll talk tomorrow."

"I shall not stop dancing until we meet again!" vowed Sheen as he danced out the door.

Back at Jimmy's house Carl was now watching television with Mr. and Mrs. Neutron.

He shyly smiled at Mrs. Neutron. "How would you like to go out to a movie, dinner, and dancing?"

"Gee, that sounds like fun!" said Mr. Neutron, jumping up. "I'll get the car!"

Carl shook his head. "Sorry, Mr. Neutron, you're not invited."
Mrs. Neutron frowned. "Carl, I think you'd better go home."
Carl winked at Mrs. Neutron. "We shall speak of this later when you-know-who isn't around."
As Carl walked out the door Mr. Neutron turned to his wife. "That is one weird kid!"

Down in Jimmy's secret lab Jimmy and Cindy were on their very first date.

Cindy was still suspicious. "Okay, Neutron, you said you loved me. What's up with that?"

Jimmy took Cindy's hand. "I think you're more gorgeous than a thousand fiery stars exploding in the atmosphere!"

Cindy blushed. "Really? Wow! No one's ever said that to me before!"

Jimmy put his arms around Cindy. "Kiss me, you fool, before I go mad!"

Cindy closed her eyes and puckered up her lips. They were about to kiss when suddenly Jimmy saw something out of the corner of his eye . . . a small door in the containment chamber was open!

"The containment chamber is open!" cried Jimmy. "We must have been exposed to the love serum! *That's* why I'm acting so crazy!"

Suddenly Jimmy remembered Carl ordering his stinky Cheese of the Month on the computer. Carl must have punched the wrong button when he logged on.

"Hey! Do you love me or not?" demanded Cindy.

"I do!" said Jimmy. "But I don't! I've got to stop this! Farewell, my lovely!"

Jimmy grabbed Cindy, shoved her into his lab-ejection chair and pressed a button. *SPROING!* Cindy landed outside.

Jimmy's mind raced to figure out how to counteract the love serum. "That's it!" he cried. "The love serum works through the sense of smell! If I can counteract the odor we won't be in love anymore!"

Jimmy spent the rest of the evening testing which bad smells blocked the love serum, but they were all too weak. Then Jimmy had a better idea.

The next day at school everything was back to normal. Well, almost. . . .

"The effects of the serum will dissipate in a week, but until then we have to wear this cheese," explained Jimmy.

"Hey, Jimmy, thanks for fixing things before I married Libby," said Sheen.

"And before I became your stepdad," said Carl.

"Don't thank me, guys," said Jimmy. "Thank Carl's Cheese of the Month Club!"